BELLA
The St. Augustine Sea Turtle

Written by Marion Matthews
Illustrated by Abigail Lashbrook

This is my second sea turtle children's book. It is dedicated to my grandchildren and the "Children of the Sea."
Grama Marion

BELLA
The St. Augustine Sea Turtle

Text and illustrations copyright 2023 by Marion Matthews.
All rights reserved.
ISBN: 978-1-7379314-2-3

Starlee the Sanibel Sea Turtle is my first children's book.
ISBN: 978-1-7379314-0-9

From the islands to the sea
Let them be wild and free
It's up to you, the children and me

Bella was born in the sand on a beautiful island, filled with seashells and palm trees.

She and her brothers and sisters were wild and happy and free. They were often seen clapping their water-wings and diving deep, down into the sea.

Then one day her mother sang out and said, "Beautiful Bella of the sea, it is time to remember your song, to grow-up and be strong. Do you remember your dream, how you sang about the city of St. Augustine? The land of the old, where it was once fortold:

A turtle born near the blue, would one day tell a story so magical, tender and true. Bella dear, could this be you?"

So Bella straightened her flippers and clicked her green-gold foot slippers. She smiled at her mother and said, "I do remember my dream about St. Augustine and a gold twinkling star! That somehow, I am connected and must travel afar.

So it is time to begin my new journey. Know that I love you all so much! I will do my best to stay in touch."

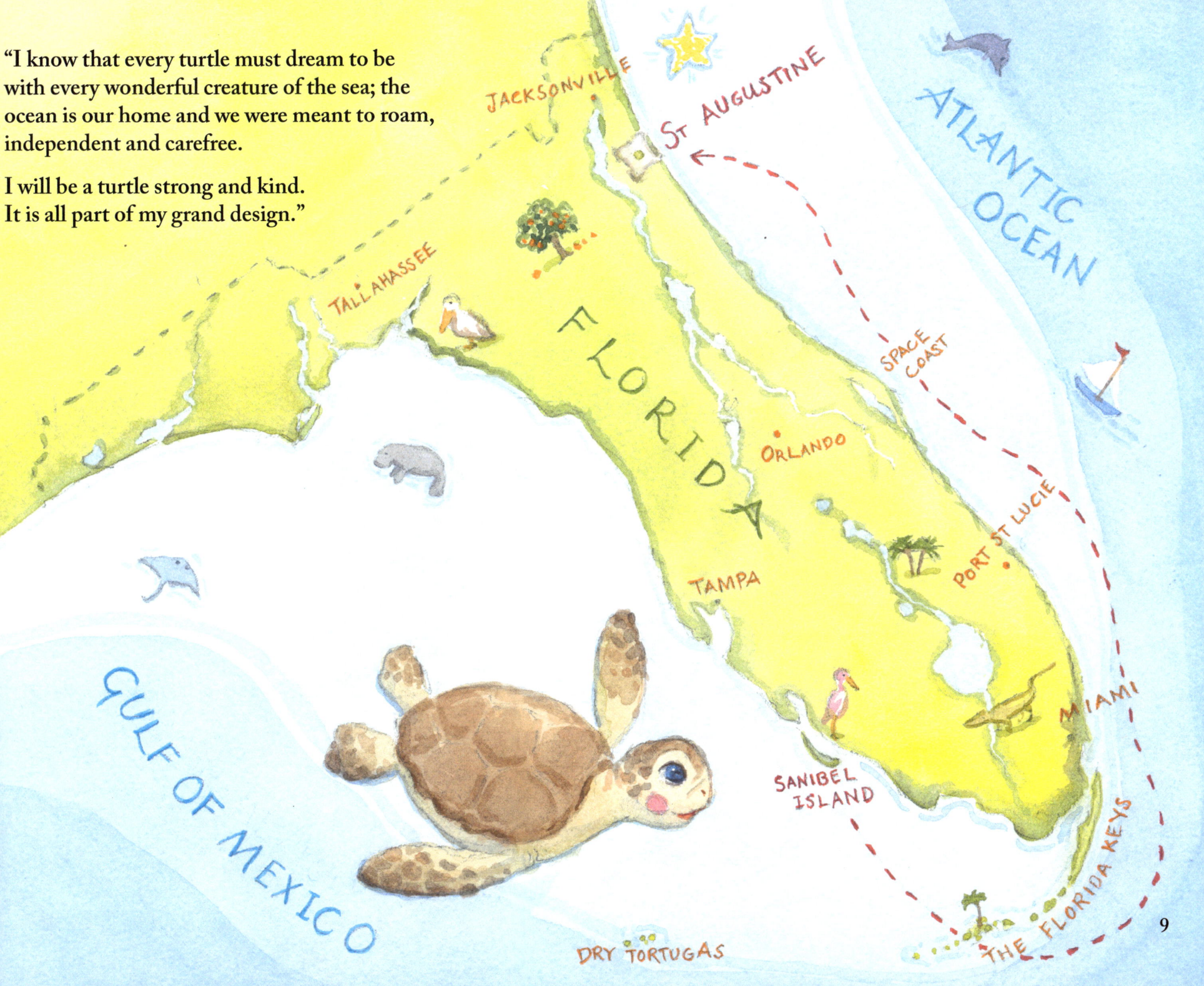

"I know that every turtle must dream to be with every wonderful creature of the sea; the ocean is our home and we were meant to roam, independent and carefree.

I will be a turtle strong and kind. It is all part of my grand design."

Bella travelled two days and a night, following that yellow blinking light. And somewhere around the Florida Keys she danced with some manatees. She then swam by Miami and turned her attention north to Port St. Lucie.

At Cocoa Beach she played with dolphins just out of reach. It was her first time to see surfers climb up on longboards, and soar like birds in the sky.

Bella laughed and said, "Hi! Would you like to race?" So they surfed and guess what? She got first place!

Then with a flip and a dip she continued to travel north.

Her star now seemed closer and brighter then ever before …

Along the Space Coast a rocket was seen taking off in the air. And she knew in her heart she was almost there! The water was beautiful, her new friends they swam by her.

Her journey was now almost complete, she just needed to get something to eat …

So she swam up to the ocean surface, the sargassum seaweed such a sweet treat. It tasted sooo good. Then she saw something odd - shiny and bright - it was a grey and metallic and did not look quite right … But she was hungry so she said to herself, "I'll just take one more bite."

She then felt a tug, what was this? Then her mouth did turn a little red. She was caught by a hook and a fishermens web.

She felt a little pain and some panic as she fought to break free. She heard the fishermen yell, "I'm so, so sorry! We must let her go!" Bella with one large tear dropped into the water below …

Some time it did pass, how long had it been? Then she heard her mother above her say in the wind, "Bella remember your song, it is not very long to the shore. Although you are hurt, it is not that bad; remember you belong to the sea and you can still be who you were meant to be… my beautiful Bella, strong, courageous and free."

So Bella brought her head to the surface, one more breath did she take; she knew she must just stay awake …

And although she was sore, she could feel that her other three flippers were strong! So with the help of the waves, and a little angel fish she named Dave, she swam harder than ever before and was washed up onto the shore.

The St. Augustine Sea Turtle Hospital

After some time sleeping Bella slowly opened her eyes. She could feel the warm soft sand and was so happy she was on dry land. Then she heard the patter of little feet …

Could this be the famous Children of the Sea who live in St. Augustine? Her heart filled with joy! And a little boy then said, "Hello, my name is Roy!"

The Children of the Sea then gathered around Bella to protect her. They called the Sea Turtle Hospital and said, "Come quickly we have found her, she is still alert, but appears to be hurt. Please, we need you to help us!"

Soon after, Bella heard people running up the beach. One of the children said, "I know this seams like a bad-dream, but don't worry, they are the Sea Turtle Hospital A-Team."

Devon, with her team of Kaylee, Keenan, Torri and Vic, then said, "We are here, do not fear and who do we have here?"

Bella then looked up as Devon wrapped her so gently, "My story I will tell you, but please thank the Children of the Sea - they are the ones who found me."

Bella soon fell asleep tucked into her soft blanket. And she heard Devon whisper, "Although you will need to stay with us for awhile, I promise you, you will return to the sand, this old land and swim deep into the sea. You will be the strong woman you were meant to be."

Devon then said, "Children of the Sea, thank you, thank you, thank you!"

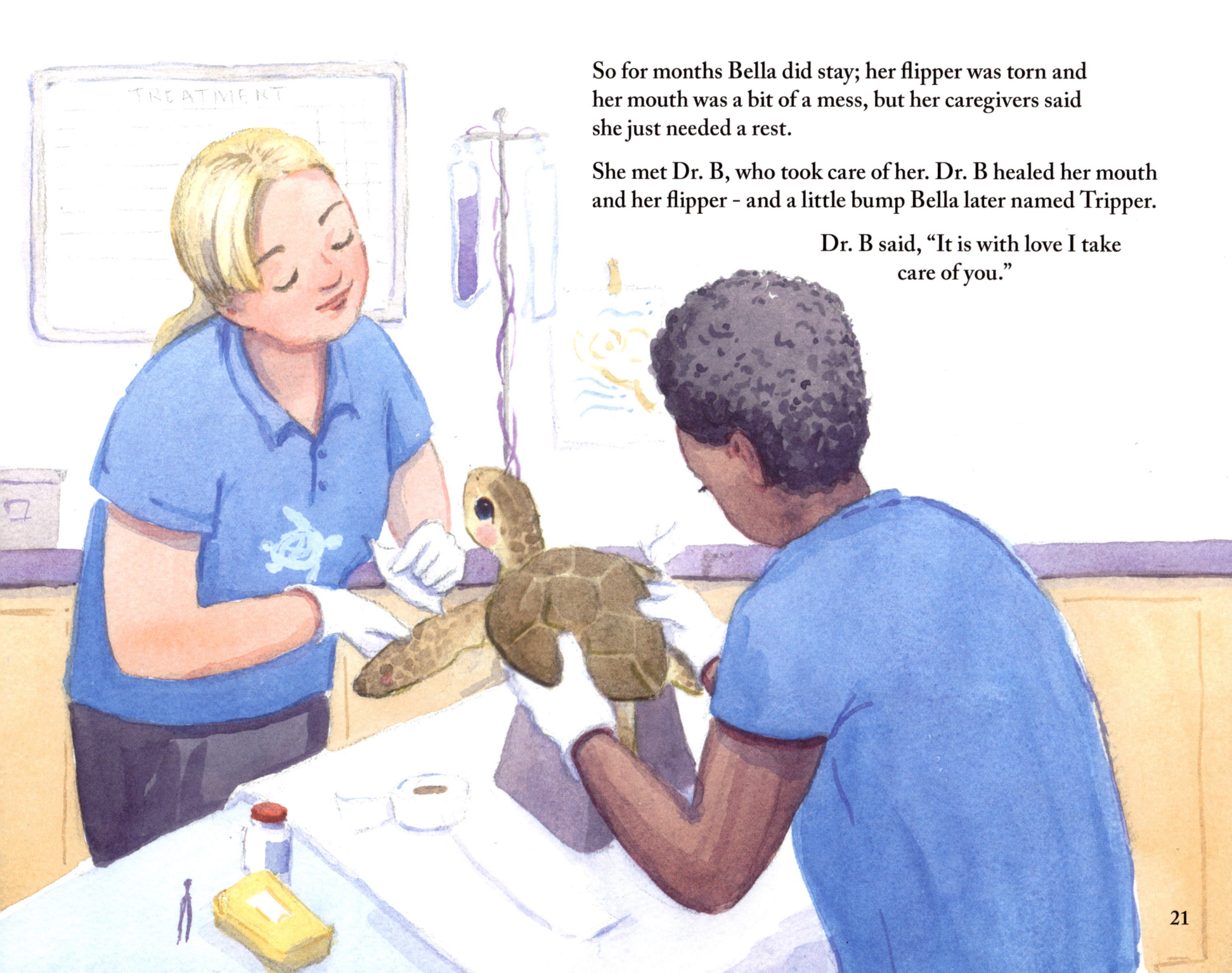

So for months Bella did stay; her flipper was torn and her mouth was a bit of a mess, but her caregivers said she just needed a rest.

She met Dr. B, who took care of her. Dr. B healed her mouth and her flipper - and a little bump Bella later named Tripper.

Dr. B said, "It is with love I take care of you."

And there was Catherine, who is nicknamed "Cat," who often sat with Bella. Cat did not say much, but Bella knew she could trust Cat.

Then one day when Bella came up for air in the tank, she saw Cat wipe a tear from her eye. Cat said, "Soon, we will have to say good-bye."

And Bella knew Cat cared so much … she cried.

Two weeks later, an old woman came by and said, "My name is Grama Marion. You may not remember for you were just a baby turtle, but I was there when you were born and crawled out of your shell on the sandy shores of Sanibel.

I am so proud of you and I have brought you good news!

You are now better, and I have a letter that says tomorrow is the day. You have been cleared to sail away; to go back into the sea – you will be set free!"

The next day Bella was released to the ocean.

She was so happy; she played and laughed and sang.

"Although nature is beautiful, it sometimes needs a hand. Without all of you, the Children of the Sea and the hospital I might have died on the sand. I will never forget St. Augustine and this special land!"

Bella and the Children of the Sea

Bella began her journey swimming near the ancient City of St. Augustine. With a wink to the dolphin who just swam by she said, "I have found my pupose; to encourage kids to be Children of the Sea, and take care of creatures just like me!"

"I will call-out and sing to the children who live here or come to visit. Go through the old city gate, don't wait! You must walk down to the fort."

"I will always be with you Children of the Sea, and please take care of turtles like me. Won't you come to the old city fort to visit me? You will hear me in the breeze saying, when you are waving …"

"We are all worth Saving!"

Bella then smiled as she looked at her favorite palm trees near the old fort walls. She waved to the children one more time. "Come back tomorrow and be with me. I love you so much!" Bella then dove down deep into the sea.

She was very happy, healthy and free.

This is the end of this wonderful story.
Won't you protect nature in all of its glory?

About the Illustrator

Abigail Lashbrook grew up taking long walks in the country, where she would look at everything and find favorite things to draw. When she got older, she went to art school and studied children's book illustration. Now she enjoys illustrating books that combine her early love for nature with compelling stories about the way the world works. She still likes to paint things she finds outside, and you can often find her hiking with a bag of drawing materials, looking for something to capture on paper for other people to see.

About the Author

Some say Grandma Marion is Marion Matthews, a protector of natural resources. Marion began her career as one of California's first women Fish and Game Wardens. She was responsible for protecting the Mojave Desert and the Southern Sierra Nevada Mountain's wild creatures from poachers and pollution. She then joined the US Forest Service to keep our Forests safe from illegal use and wildfire. In recent years Marion helped train Park Rangers and taught college Environmental Conservation. This is her second book. Rumor has it that Grandma Marion can sometimes be seen walking along the Fort walls and talking to Bella.

This is the second children's book written by Marion Matthews, dedicated to her grandchildren and the Children of the Sea.

Her first book is *Starlee the Sanibel Sea Turtle*.
ISBN: 978-1-7379314-0-9

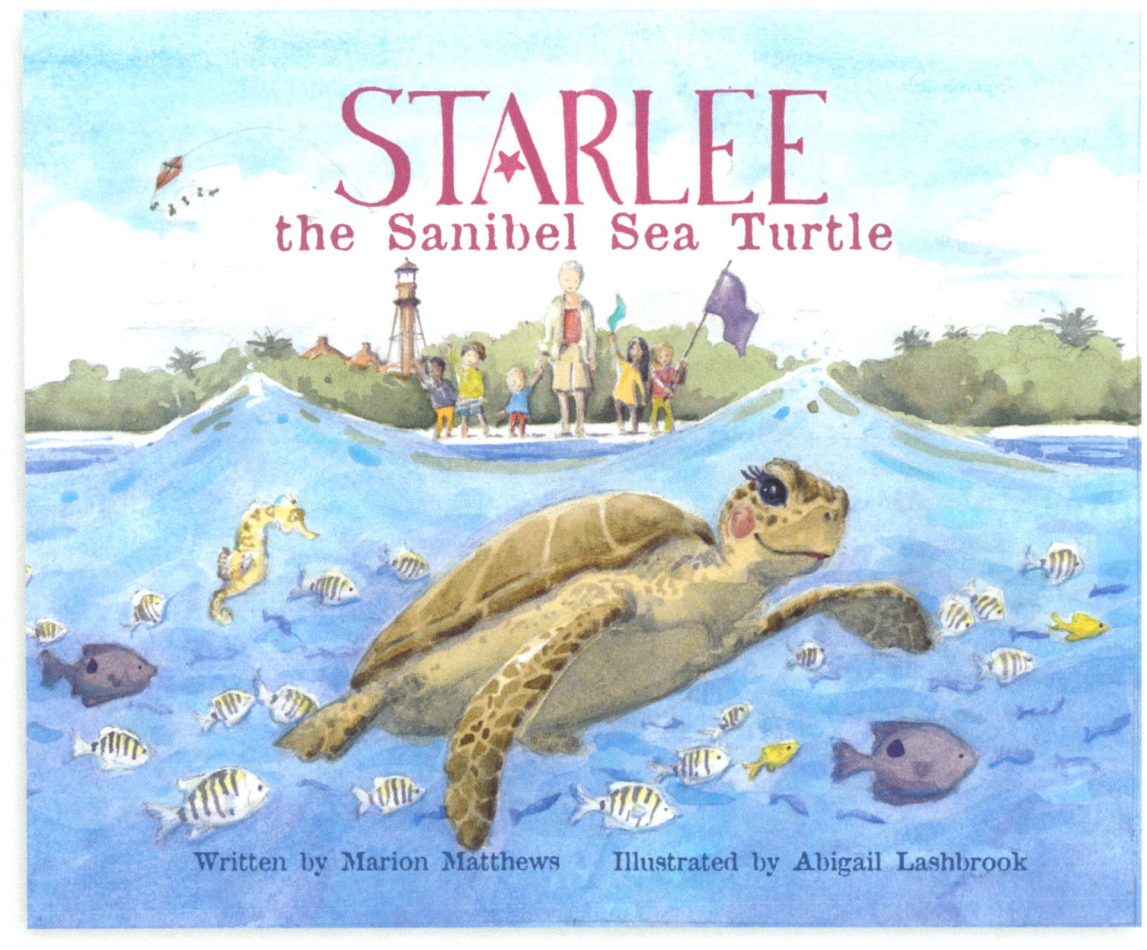

Printed in the USA
CPSIA information can be obtained
at www.ICGtesting.com
LVHW062234271123
764330LV00002B/1